SCRATCH N SNITCH

EVAN JACOBS

SADDLEBACK
EDUCATIONAL PUBLISHING

BREAK AND ENTER

IGGY

ON THE RUN

QWIK CUTTER

REBEL

SCRATCH N' SNITCH

EDUCATIONAL PUBLISHING
www.sdlback.com

ISBN-13: 978-1-68021-104-7
ISBN-10: 1-68021-104-8
eBook: 978-1-63078-421-8

Printed in Guangzhou, China
NOR/1015/CA21501554

20 19 18 17 16   1 2 3 4 5

STATS AT MARINA MIDDLE SCHOOL

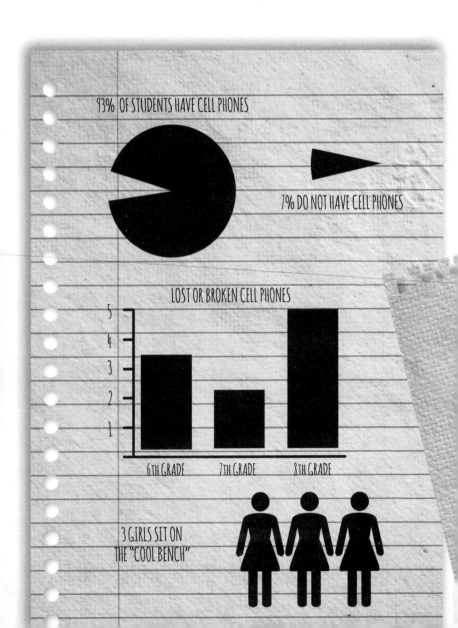

93% OF STUDENTS HAVE CELL PHONES

7% DO NOT HAVE CELL PHONES

LOST OR BROKEN CELL PHONES

5
4
3
2
1

6TH GRADE   7TH GRADE   8TH GRADE

3 GIRLS SIT ON
THE "COOL BENCH"

EASY REPAIR

HARD REPAIR

ME, ME, AND ME

Mia Gonzalez walked over to the "cool" bench. You had to be cool to hang there. She saw Cassidy and Nicole. They were her besties at Marina Middle School. The cool bench was in the center of campus. The girls stood there so everybody could see them. They were picture-perfect. Always.

The three girls were the coolest eighth graders at school. Mia was a goddess, with her long brown hair and tanned skin. Cassidy and Nicole made her shine. Both had blonde hair and fair skin. Mia "popped" in between.

The three girls got straight As. They didn't have to study hard. Or work much.

Mia was the most popular. Kids envied Cassidy and Nicole. But Mia had a way about her that went beyond them.

Mia knew she was cool. And that wasn't a good thing.

She was spoiled.

She was self-centered.

She was selfish.

She was just about every bad "self" word you could be.

She had been popular since first grade. Nobody challenged her. Everybody accepted how she was.

Mia got within a few feet of the cool bench. Deemed cool by her, naturally. She saw something that made her jaw drop. Two boys were standing next to it. Her bench! They were too close for comfort.

"What's up with the losers?" she asked Cassidy and Nicole.

As usual, the girls had their phones. They were always holding them. Always taking selfies. And posting. They *were* their phones.

"We thought we'd let you handle it." Cassidy grinned. Then she checked her phone.

"Yeah, you're better at dealing with losers than we are," Nicole said.

"I know." Mia smiled smugly.

She walked over to the two boys. They wore hoodies. Skinny jeans. Vans. They had long hair. And they held skateboards.

All Mia saw were two kids who were less than she was.

Less good-looking. Less popular. Less smart. Why? Because she thought they were.

"Gross," Mia said when she got closer. "Why don't you two take your discussion somewhere else." It wasn't a question.

They both stared at her.

"You're too close to the cool bench." She pointed to it. Rolled her eyes. Cassidy and Nicole giggled.

"We're not even near—" one boy started to say.

"Listen," Mia snapped. "I'm a person. You're a person. But I'm a *better* person. Everybody knows this bench is ours. So, why don't you two go somewhere else? Sit at the lunch tables with the other skaters."

The boys had no reply. They stared at Mia. Then they walked away.

Mia sniffed. Mission accomplished. She noticed some posters for the Zombie Dance that Friday. The school hosted the dance the week before Halloween every year. Mia and her boyfriend, Neil, hadn't talked about going. They didn't have to. She knew he would take her.

Neil went to Ocean High School. He was one of the few sophomores on the varsity football team. He was tall. And he looked like a surfer, with a muscular build and wavy blond hair.

Mia turned to Cassidy and Nicole. She was grinning as her phone buzzed with an incoming text. She knew it was Neil. He always texted her first thing in the morning.

NEIL: (Hang out later?)
MIA: (Maybe.)

She figured they would hang out. She wanted to. But she didn't want to seem too eager. Mia knew guys liked girls more when they had to work for it. Chase them.

"Who was that?" Cassidy asked.

"Neil." Mia shrugged. She liked not caring. Or at least looking like she didn't care.

The bell rang.

"Time to be bored." Mia rolled her eyes.

The girls followed her. They had classes in

the opposite direction. But they always walked Mia to her first class.

As they went, it seemed like all eyes were on them. Students moved out of their way. The girls liked parading around the campus.

They did get smiles from Rand, Donovan, and Jeff as they passed. They were eighth graders too. They liked to dress preppy—1980s all the way. They wore topsiders. Polo shirts. Dress pants. They even combed their hair like guys did in the '80s. They were as popular as Mia, Cassidy, and Nicole.

Then the Scabs walked by.

CHAPTER 2

WHATEVER

Something smells. Oh my God!" Mia laughed. Cassidy and Nicole did too.

The Scabs kept walking. If they heard Mia's comment, they didn't say anything. The popular kids ignored the Scabs.

The Scabs were Lori, Viet, Logan, and Tom. They dressed in black every day. They wore T-shirts with the names of metal bands. They also wore jackets or hoodies, even when it was a million degrees outside.

"They don't look like boys *or* girls!" Mia had joked. She mocked Lori and Viet's short hair. Mia would never cut her hair so short.

Mia, Cassidy, and Nicole had been in school with the Scabs since first grade. They had never gotten along. Well, Mia had never liked them. She thought they were lazy, stupid, and gross.

"They're scabs!" she had said in the fourth grade. "They don't do anything."

The name stuck.

Mia was always rolling her eyes at them. She thought they were troublemakers. She disliked what they wore. And sometimes she just couldn't stand the sight of them. But she still had to take classes with the Scabs.

One of the classes was PE.

It was fourth period. The sport was basketball. Everyone was playing. Everyone except Mia and Cassidy. Mia had sweet-talked Coach Fife. She told him her legs hurt. She gave him a pained look.

Teachers weren't supposed to play favorites. But Mia won him over. He told her she could hang out near the gym's bleachers and skip class.

"But then I'll be alone," Mia said, pouting. "Can't Cassidy come with me? For moral support? Please?"

"Okay," Coach Fife said.

The sound of basketballs bouncing on the floor echoed in the gym. Mia and Cassidy were perched against the folded bleachers. They were standing behind one of the baskets.

The girls laughed as they shared photos. Normally, students weren't allowed to have their phones out during class. During lunch, snack, and between classes it was okay. Coach Fife hadn't said anything about it. So they figured, why not?

Mia loved Instagram. It was her favorite social media site. She loved seeing what people posted. The girls would spend hours viewing the app.

Mia and Cassidy didn't notice Lori and Viet

playing basketball with some other girls. Even though they were right in front of them.

"He's so lame," Mia said. Cassidy showed her a photo on Zach Perez's Instagram page.

Zach was the school nerd. He tucked in his shirts. His pants were too high. He was always messing around on his iPad. He was not cool. He was into "the science of computers," as he liked to say. He was also a year younger, a lowly seventh grader.

"Why does he even have a page?" Cassidy asked. "He only has four followers."

"Probably his mom, his dad, his brother … and you," Mia joked. She enjoyed teasing Cassidy and Nicole sometimes. They never teased her back.

Mia set her phone down on the gym floor. She picked up her bottled water. Then took a sip. As she looked up, Lori was running toward her. She had lost control of the basketball.

It smashed down on Mia's phone.

Crunch!

Lori put her hands out. She landed against the bleachers. She had come within inches of hitting Mia.

"What are you doing?" Mia yelled.

"Sorry," Lori said. She grabbed the ball and started to walk away.

"Oh my God," Cassidy screamed. "She broke your phone!"

Mia's body went cold. Not her phone. She used it for everything.

She picked it up. It looked like a brick had fallen on it. The screen was scratched. The glass had a crack in the center. Even worse? The scratch ran across her home screen.

"You're gonna pay for this," Mia said. She got up and ran over to Coach Fife. "Lori wrecked my phone," she said. She held it up so Coach Fife could see.

Lori and Viet followed.

"Why are you snitching?" Viet asked.

"It was an accident," Lori said.

"If it was an accident, then I'm not snitching." Mia moved the phone even closer to the coach's face. "Does this scratch look like an accident? And look at this crack. It's ruined!"

Mia was furious. Why were the Scabs upset? It was their fault.

"It was on the ground," Lori said. "Why'd she put it there?"

"Do PE like everyone else! Then this never would've happened," Viet said.

"Whether they join the class or not is none of your concern," Coach Fife said.

"Yeah," Mia said. "Mind your own business, Scab!"

"Now, Mia, calm down." Coach Fife looked at her sternly. "Lori, you need to go to the office."

"Why? It was an accident," Lori protested.

"Because you broke Mia's phone."

"She didn't break it. Why was Mia on her

phone anyway? Students aren't supposed to have them out during class," Viet said.

"Go to the office now." Coach Fife folded his arms. He stood closer to Mia, as if he were protecting her.

Lori and Viet started walking across the gym.

"I'm satisfied." Mia's anger was completely gone. "Hopefully Principal Lyon will get her parents to pay for my phone. Mine can totally afford it. But why should they pay?"

Mia moved close to Cassidy. She saw Lori and Viet look back at her.

"Keep going!" Mia waved.

Lori turned and glared at her.

"Buh-bye," Mia said.

"She looked like she was going to get you later," Cassidy said.

"Get me? The only thing she's going to get is expelled from school."

Mia checked her phone. It still worked. She sighed with relief.

Her phone was okay. That was what mattered. Not being able to use it because of the Scabs? That would have been a disaster.

CHAPTER 3

L IS FOR LOSER

Come on, Ann," Mia yelled in front of the entire tennis team. "Serve it harder!"

She was at tennis practice. She was part of a private after-school tennis team. They practiced twice a week. Like everything she put her mind to, Mia was a good tennis player. She hit harder than the other girls. She had more energy. And she never gave up.

Today, she was in a practice game against

the worst player on the team. Ann wasn't fast. She didn't hit the ball hard. Even worse, she cried when she was under pressure.

Ann hadn't cried today. And she had already lost two sets to Mia. She was about to lose her third. She hadn't scored any points.

Ann served the ball. Mia slammed it back. Ann missed.

The match was over.

"Both of you played very well out there," Coach Austin said.

The girls walked off the court.

Mia looked across the parking lot. Her mom had pulled up in her SUV.

"Wow!" Ann said. "You're, like, really good."

She hadn't even noticed Ann standing next to her.

"I know," Mia said without smiling. "You should be good too. With how much we practice. But you're not meant to play tennis."

She walked away before Ann could respond.

She didn't think about how she had insulted Ann. This was just how Mia was. How she had always been.

Mia's mom was fashionably dressed, just like her daughter. She handed Mia a sweet icy drink once she got in the car.

"Mom!" Mia said as she pushed the drink away. "I can't drink that. It'll make me feel bloated and fat. I told you, always get me an iced-tea."

"Well." Mia's mother smiled. "I thought just this once …" She attempted to hand it back to Mia. She pushed it away again, harder.

"How about never? Iced-tea, Mom. That's all you're allowed to get me from Starbucks." Mia picked up her phone. "Do I need to text it to you? I want you to remember."

"No, Mia. I don't think you need to go that far." Her mother put the drink in the cup holder. "But I think you're being rude."

"Whatever."

Mia started texting Neil. He was coming over

later. She couldn't wait to tell him the story about how her phone got damaged.

"Mia?" Neil asked. "Are you even listening?"

She wasn't. She was too busy taking photos of her dog, Corky. He was a brown dachshund. They were in the living room of her house. The room was big. It held two large couches. There was a big coffee table. For family fun there was a seventy-inch flat-screen TV over the fireplace. There were large plants in the corners and expensive art on the walls.

Mia's parents were in the kitchen making dinner.

"You didn't hear anything I said. About football practice," Neil said. "You didn't hear about how Coach benched me for the next game. I missed a pass in practice."

"You'll catch another pass," Mia said.

She continued to click away on her camera. She tried to get Corky to do cute things. She hoped one of the photos turned out. She wanted to post it to her Instagram account. No matter what, she was going to Snapchat it to Cassidy and Nicole.

Neil took out his iPad. Mia glanced at it for a second. He was reading *To Kill a Mockingbird* on it.

"This book is dope," Neil said. "Do you know anything about it?"

"No. And I don't want to."

"It was written a long time ago. But it's really good. It's about this girl, Scout. Her dad, Atticus, is a lawyer—"

"Why are you telling me about it?" Mia snapped.

"Because it's really good."

"I'll hear about it next year when I'm at Ocean. Besides, Neil, that book is so old. Like, if you want me to be interested in reading something? If you want me to be interested in anything you say? Have it matter to me."

"I listened to your whole story about that stupid phone," he yelled. "*It* didn't matter to *me*."

"You don't care that a gross Scab scratched my phone?" She was starting to get mad about what happened at school all over again.

"I didn't say that." Neil tried to change his tone. "I just think you should be more open-minded. Give more things a chance."

"Maybe you should leave." She opened up a game of Candy Crush on her phone.

"I thought I was eating over," he said.

"You were." She didn't take her eyes off the game.

Neil put his iPad in his backpack.

"Later, Mia," he said as he walked out. He slammed the door behind him.

Her mom walked into the living room. She still wore oven mitts.

Mia didn't say anything.

"Uh, Mia," her mother said. "I thought Neil was staying for dinner."

"Oh, him?" Mia still didn't look up from her game. "He left."

"Was he upset? I heard the door slam."

"Maybe. But he'll get over it. He likes me."

Mia continued to play Candy Crush. She didn't even notice when her mom left the room.

CHAPTER 4

OKAY, THIS IS A JOKE

Mia was comfortably in bed. She didn't want to get up. She snuggled into her pink blanket. Corky repositioned himself on her feet.

She opened her eyes. Then looked around the room. She was surrounded by photographs. Some were taken at the mall. Others were taken at Disneyland. A few were from school. Cassidy and Nicole were in a few. But most of them were only of Mia.

She also had posters of All Time Low, One Direction, Led Zeppelin, and Mumford and Sons.

She closed her eyes.

Her phone buzzed. It was a text from Cassidy. She could tell by the sound. She grabbed it off the nightstand. She hated having to look at it through the scratched screen. She couldn't even look at the center crack. *Stupid Scabs*, she thought.

Last night she had pitched a fit. Her dad had said he was too busy to take her to the mall to get the phone fixed. There were kiosks that could replace the screen in an hour. Her dad promised they would go tonight.

CASSIDY: OMG! Have u seen Instagram?

MIA: No.

CASSIDY: See this.

Cassidy sent her a link.

Mia clicked on it.

That's when she saw the post. It was a photo. One she had never seen before.

Even worse?

In it she was making out with Zach!

Four-eyes Zach.

Drooling Zach.

Somebody had taken two photos. Then put them together.

One of Mia.

One of Zach.

It looked real. This would be a problem.

"What?!" she cried as she sat up.

She was so loud even Corky looked up. The cozy warmth of her bedroom disappeared.

She quickly reported the image as "inappropriate." This made her feel good, for about a half-second. She knew Instagram had a process. They weren't going to take down a post so easily.

She eyed the clock on her dresser. It was six thirty.

School would start in less than an hour.

Mia quickly scrolled around on her phone. In her shock she hadn't even looked at who posted the photo.

It had come from Zach's account. That's why

Cassidy had sent her the link. Mia never looked at his account. She didn't follow him. And didn't want to.

"Zach!" she yelled.

Corky barked.

"Shhh!"

She gritted her teeth. She clenched her fists. Her mind started working overtime.

What am I gonna do when more people see this? What if Neil sees it? Oh no! What if it goes viral?

"Wait," she said out loud. "Don't panic. Just get ahead of it. Like they do on TV."

She got out of bed. Then took a quick shower. She didn't even bother to shampoo her hair. She washed her hair daily. But not today. It wasn't worth the time. She needed to strategize.

Mia thought about what to do while getting ready. She made sure she looked great. Then she grabbed her backpack. She took the stairs two at a time. She opened the front door—

"Mia," her mom yelled. She was in the

kitchen. Mia could hear breakfast cooking. She noticed the smell of bacon frying.

"You haven't eaten breakfast," her mom said. She was near the front door now.

"But, Mom," Mia said.

"You're not leaving without eating." Her tone was stern.

Mia didn't feel like arguing. She didn't want to be grounded. Not with the Zombie Dance happening this weekend. Her parents rarely punished her. But she wasn't taking any chances. Not with what was happening on Instagram. She went to the kitchen. Then she sat down at the table.

"You're quiet this morning," her mother said, handing her a bowl of cereal. "You're not even texting."

Mia grabbed her phone. She didn't have any messages. That was weird.

None from Cassidy or Nicole. Not even one from Neil. She wondered if she was still cool. She wondered if the fake photo had ruined her status. Was she still queen of Marina Middle School?

Yeah, right! You bet I am. She smiled to herself. She felt a little better. Still, it was weird to doubt herself. She never doubted herself.

She texted Cassidy.

MIA: (That pic! No words. What the …)
CASSIDY: (300 likes already! ;-))

Mia's body went limp. Her phone slipped from her hand. What was happening? She took a deep breath.

It seemed like Cassidy was smiling behind those words. Enjoying the moment. Having fun at Mia's expense.

Is everybody laughing at me now? Wait. Stop doubting yourself, Mia thought.

She eyed her cereal. She wanted to eat some. And she knew her mom would ask questions if she didn't.

She didn't want to talk about it. She didn't want to talk about anything. She scooped some of the cereal into her mouth. And she forced herself to swallow.

It didn't make her feel any better. She closed her eyes. Took another breath.

"Honey, is everything okay?" Her mother came over and felt her head. "You're losing color by the second."

"I'm fine," Mia said.

She quickly stood up. And grabbed her backpack. Then she left the house. She had to get out of there. What if her mom asked more questions? She might make her stay home.

Maybe today was shaping up to be the worst day of Mia's life. But there was no way she was going to miss it.

CHAPTER 5

ALL RIGHT, THIS ISN'T FUNNY

Mia made her way over to the cool bench. She was nervous. It wasn't because she felt like everybody was looking at her. She loved that. It was *why* she felt like they were looking at her.

They know about the picture, she thought, panicking. *They really think I kissed disgusting Zach.*

She kept walking. She moved past the rockers. The hipsters. The preppies. The punkers. The jocks. Normally, she didn't notice these kids. Today, she noticed everyone.

All she had to do was get to the cool bench. It would protect her. Everyone would see she was still awesome.

What to do about that stupid image? She would figure it out later.

Mia checked Instagram. The bogus photo was still up. It had close to one thousand likes. What?! How was that possible?

"Ugh!" she groaned. Mia tried to keep her composure. She wanted to scream.

Eventually, she met up with Cassidy and Nicole. She'd made it to the bench.

"Instagram is blowing up," Cassidy said with a sly smile.

"Yeah," Nicole said.

They seemed happy. Mia wanted to yell at them. Set them straight. Let them know whoever had posted that photo was going to pay.

Pay!

But she didn't.

"I can't believe Zach would do this," Mia said. "I've never done anything to him."

Cassidy and Nicole didn't say anything. They didn't back her up. They didn't tell her everything would be okay.

"He's kinda cute," Cassidy said with a laugh.

Nicole laughed too.

Her blood boiled. Why were her best friends enjoying this?

Before she could ask, Cassidy and Nicole walked away.

"What?" Mia said under her breath.

How dare they do this! she thought. *I'm the leader. I rule this school.*

She followed them. She never did this. It was just not done. Cassidy and Nicole were *always* behind her.

"You guys don't think this is funny, do

you? How would you feel if that were you in the picture?" she asked. Mia was trying not to sound desperate. Or pathetic.

"Calm down," Cassidy said without looking at her. "Everybody still loves you."

"For now," Nicole said.

Then they laughed at her.

Again.

The bell rang. The two girls walked off to first period. They both had art.

Mia's next class was math.

She felt so alone. What was happening?

During math, Mia couldn't focus. Mr. Dalton had given them time to do the homework assignment in class. He was letting kids use the calculator app on their phones. Students loved it. That made it easier to text or check social media.

Mia felt like all eyes were on her. That everybody was texting about her.

She didn't know what they were saying.

Maybe she didn't want to know.

When there was a laugh? She thought it was about her. When she heard a whisper? She thought it was about the Instagram photo.

Her emotions kept building.

The looks.

The laughs.

The talk.

She couldn't take it. She stood up, fuming. Then she stormed out of the classroom.

"Mia!" Mr. Dalton called out after her.

But she was gone.

Mia walked toward the school's playing field. She was going to the PE class. She would confront Zach.

She knew he had PE first period. Mia had seen him running there when the bell rang. His arms flailing. His legs moving in different directions.

Awkward! He's such a dork, she thought.

She made her way to the track. Some students

were running. Others were walking. Some were playing football. A few were doing long jumps.

Mia easily spotted Zach. He was running around the track. Did he have any coordination? His arms and legs jerked awkwardly. Or so it seemed to her.

"I need to confront that nerd," she said under her breath.

She knew she was acting like a crazy person. But she didn't care. She walked over to him.

"Who do you think you are?" she yelled. "Do you think it's funny? Posting a picture like that! Why did you do it? You know I'd never *ever* kiss you. Not in a million-trillion years."

"What are you talking about?" Zach asked.

"You know what, Zach?" Mia started talking slower. She wanted her words to hurt more. "You're ugly. Nobody at this school likes you. You're just a gross—"

"Hey!" Mrs. Minna, the seventh-grade PE

teacher, approached. She got between them. "Who do you think you are? You can't talk that way. Not at this school. Not with disrespect."

Mrs. Minna was new to the school. She was tall. She had long blonde hair. Even though she was strict, students liked her. And not just because she was pretty.

"Take that disgusting picture down!" Mia poked her finger on Zach's shoulder. Then she turned to leave.

Mrs. Minna blocked her.

"You need to go to the principal's office, young lady," she said.

Mia glared at her.

"This has nothing to do with you!" Mia said harshly. "Why don't you go blow your whistle or something? You obviously don't know who I am."

Mrs. Minna took a deep breath.

"You're right. I don't know who you are. So

I'm going to walk you to the office myself. Then I'll find out."

The teacher took Mia's arm. She led her off the field.

CHAPTER 6

WHAT?

I really am sorry," Mia said. She looked at Principal Lyon. She felt bad for yelling at Mrs. Minna. But not at Zach.

Mia had been angry with Mrs. Minna. However, as she walked to the principal's office, she calmed down. She realized she was in big trouble. She had been disrespectful. This day was already weird enough. She didn't need to get suspended.

Mrs. Lyon was a elegant woman. Her hair was perfect. And she wore a pantsuit that made her look corporate. Mia had heard her parents say she was the youngest principal in Mia's school district.

"I don't know what came over me," Mia said.

"I'm going to let you off this time. But with a warning, Miss Gonzalez," the principal said. "But, please. Remember this in the future. You're a leader at this school. Act like it. No more outbursts. And you need to apologize to Mrs. Minna."

Mia breathed a sigh of relief. As she left the office, her phone buzzed. It was a text from Neil.

He sent her the fake photo. His text was simple.

NEIL: (?)

She started to respond. But a campus security guard walked by. Mia quickly put her phone away.

It was best to go back to first-period math. She didn't need more trouble.

The day continued to be odd.

She still felt like people were looking at her. She knew they were talking about the photo. Many kids had phones. She saw a lot of them on their phones. Each time, she assumed they were talking about her. She tried to focus on her work. But she couldn't.

Cassidy and Nicole continued to act coldy at lunch. They weren't at the cool bench. She finally found them by the blacktop. They didn't seem happy to see her. They were talking about going to the mall after school.

And they didn't invite her.

What's going on? Mia wanted to scream.

But she couldn't. Especially after her visit to the principal.

As the school day ended, Mia left. Alone (another thing that never happened)! Her phone buzzed with a text. Another from Neil.

NEIL: Looks like ur going to Zombie dance with Zach. Consider us broken up.

Mia couldn't believe what she was reading. She was upset. She was in a daze. Literally. The Scabs passed by her. She didn't even notice.

CHAPTER 7

HUH?

Mia decided to go to the mall. She wanted to find Cassidy and Nicole. She had to talk to them. Why were things so weird between them? They were her besties. They should be there for her.

It can't be because of that picture, she told herself. *Has it really ruined my life? Maybe they forgot to invite me. They probably think I'm gonna hang out with Neil.*

She was going to tell them what Neil did. How

dare he dump her! They would want to console her. They were her friends, right?

As she walked, she had another thought. She hoped Sam would be at the mall. He was tall and buff. Another high school football player. He was as hot as Neil, but funnier. He always tried to get her attention. He cracked a lot of jokes. He said he liked her laugh.

Mia was going to give Sam all the attention he wanted.

When she got to the mall, she went to the food court. This was where students from local schools always hung out. She walked down the steps. Her jaw practically hit the floor. She couldn't believe what she saw next.

Sam was sitting with Nicole. He had obviously just told a joke. Nicole was laughing.

Those are my laughs! Mia thought.

But it was Cassidy who shocked her. She was making the situation ugly. She was sharing an ice-cream sundae. With Neil!

This has to be a joke, she told herself. *There's no way this is happening. This day cannot get any worse!*

Mia marched over to them. She had so many things she wanted to say. So many things she wanted to do. She couldn't believe her horrible day. It was still going downhill.

Cassidy, Neil, Nicole, and Sam didn't notice her standing there.

Then Cassidy's eyes got big. It looked like she was scared.

"Finally," Mia said with a smirk. She readied for a fight.

"Brain freeze!" Cassidy laughed as she put her hand on her head.

Neil laughed too. He rubbed his hand on her head.

"Is that better?" he asked.

"Uh-oh. Hi, Mia," Nicole said.

Mia didn't know what to say. Was Nicole making fun of her?

You were always the third wheel, Mia thought. *Guys chose you after being shut down by me first. Cassidy second.*

"So," Mia said. "What's going on here?"

"Just having ice cream," Neil said as he scooped up some hot fudge.

"Yeah." Cassidy smiled. "Where's Zach?"

"Are you guys crazy?" Mia screamed. "Do you actually think that fake picture is real?"

"We're not thinking about you at all," Neil said.

Then Cassidy started to laugh. Nicole followed. Soon Neil was laughing. Then Sam.

They got louder. And louder.

Mia looked around. It seemed like everybody in the food court was laughing at her!

She turned and ran.

CHAPTER 8

PULEEZE

Mia couldn't wipe away her tears fast enough.

She felt a little better once she got outside. She didn't see anybody around. She was glad nobody could see her crying.

She made her way home. She walked through neighborhoods close to the mall. She told herself to stop thinking about what had happened. Maybe she had stepped into a weird time warp. Maybe another Mia Gonzalez was having a normal day.

That Mia was still the queen of the school. Maybe she was trapped in an alternate universe.

That's stupid, she told herself.

But she couldn't stop thinking about the day.

The photo of her and Zach.

Cassidy and Nicole blowing her off.

Being sent to the principal's office.

That was enough bad luck for an entire year.

But then Neil broke up with her.

And his rebound girlfriend was Cassidy?

And Sam was into Nicole?

"Ewww!" Mia yelled. "Yuck!"

She realized she had nothing. No friends. No boyfriend. Nobody to take her to the Zombie Dance.

Just like that, her life at school was over.

She took out her phone. But what could she do with it? There were no selfies to take. Nothing to post. No social media sites she wanted to check.

"Mia," Rand called as he rode his bike up next to her.

Mia was in her head. She didn't see him until he was beside her.

She smiled. She knew Cassidy and Nicole thought he was cute. But he had a girlfriend. She lived in a different state. Still, Mia knew Rand had always liked her.

"Hi, Rand," Mia said. She checked him out. "What's up?"

"Not much." He smiled.

She thought he was good-looking.

"What about that photo of you and Zach?"

"Oh, forget that." Mia moved closer to him. She had to do something to turn this day around. "Wanna go to the Zombie Dance together?"

She knew this would burn Cassidy up. The thought made her smile inside. She didn't care if Cassidy and Nicole were her friends. They were being mean to her.

"What about Neil?"

"Oh, him? We broke up."

Rand nodded. He seemed to be thinking about something.

"You know, Mia," he said. "I think you're really pretty. But that picture? Let's see what the fallout is. Maybe we can hang out after it gets taken down."

Mia's eyes were wide with fury. "Argh!" she screamed as she walked away from him.

"Hey, honey." Mia's dad smiled.

He had just pulled his car into the driveway.

"Hey," Mia said. She was still in a daze.

"Well," her father said. "Aren't we supposed to get your phone fixed this afternoon? Get a new screen …"

Mia's phone. Her scratched and cracked phone. She hadn't even thought about it.

"We can do it tomorrow," she said. The mall was the last place she wanted to be.

"What?" Her father seemed shocked. "Are you feeling okay? Don't you want to get it repaired?"

"It's not that big a deal." Mia walked into the house. Her father followed behind her. She didn't want to go anywhere. This day had been so embarrassing. And humbling. If that meant she had a scratched phone for a little longer, so be it.

Her mom was sitting at the kitchen table, reading. Mia could smell dinner cooking in the crockpot.

Mia sighed. "Everything's still normal," she said under her breath. Food was cooking. Her parents were home.

"You're home late. Did you go somewhere with the girls?" her mother asked.

"Barely," Mia mumbled. "Gotta do some homework, bye." It had been a long day. She felt like lying down.

As she went, she heard her parents talking.

"She didn't want to get it fixed?" Her mother sounded concerned.

"No. It's the weirdest thing," her father said.

She wanted to tell them it wasn't weird. She

could wait to have her phone fixed. But she didn't say anything. She'd had enough confrontations for one day.

She got to her room. She looked at her phone. The fake photo was still there. Mia checked her email. There was nothing from Instagram. Nothing. When would they take it down?

Her mind went crazy.

What if this was a big plot to destroy her? Unseat her as the ruling queen. What if Cassidy and Nicole were in on it? What if Instagram was in on it? What if she had ruled Marina Middle School for too long? What if—

"Time for dinner," Mia's mother called.

She looked at Corky. He was asleep on her bed. She wished she could be him. *His life is so simple*, she thought.

She sat at the dinner table. She hadn't eaten anything. Her parents talked about their day. They didn't notice her full plate. They didn't notice she was quiet.

They don't notice me at all, she thought.

"How come you guys aren't talking to me?" she blurted out.

Mia's parents looked at her, surprised.

"You *want* to talk with us?" her mother asked.

"Yeah," Mia said. "Why wouldn't I want to talk with you? You're my parents."

"Well, honey." Her dad cleared his throat. "You always seem like you're in your own world."

"That's true. You're always texting. We try and talk with you. Ask about your day. But you ignore us," her mother said.

"Oh …" Mia didn't know what to say. She knew she could be self-absorbed. Wait! She felt bad. Had she really been so awful?

"We'd love to talk with you," her father said sincerely.

"We would," her mother agreed.

"How was your day?" her dad asked.

"It was okay," Mia lied.

She just told them about her classes. She left

out the bad parts. She didn't feel like reliving the worst day of her life.

Mia finished her math homework. After such a draining day, it was nice to think about numbers. But even this felt wrong.

She hated math.

As she worked through the problems, she had an idea. *I need to confront all this stuff head-on,* she told herself. *And I need to be nicer about it.*

Tomorrow at school, Mia would talk with Zach. *He started this. Maybe he can fix it.*

Mia told herself to talk with him at the cool bench. If people saw, it was bound to "cool" Zach up. People might not think he was so dorky. Even better, they might not think she was no longer cool.

Anybody who thinks I'm stuck up won't think that anymore. That picture will have to come down.

She was desperate. She would try anything to get back to being who she thought she was.

CHAPTER 9

OKAY, GOD, MAKE THIS JOKE END

Mia checked her phone. She was walking to the back of the school. Zach always ate lunch there by himself. He was always on his iPad. He didn't seem to mind being alone.

She realized she had never been to this part of campus. It seemed to be the place for the uncool.

Band geeks. Choir nerds. Computer dorks. You name it, they were here.

Mia noticed they seemed happy. They were

talking and laughing. They were acting just like the cool kids at the front of campus. They didn't look like they were missing anything by being here.

She didn't want to meet Zach out back. Mia had wanted to do it at the cool bench. But maintenance was working there today. Nobody could go near it.

Well, she thought. *Nothing else has been going right. Why should this?*

She pressed a button on her phone. A photo of her and Neil came up. The scratch ran across the center of his face.

Good! Mia thought. She liked that it made him look ugly. That was why she kept the photo on her phone. Maybe she would wait even longer to get it fixed.

"Are you gonna scream at me again?" Zach asked as she walked up.

He was sitting on a low wall. His iPad was resting on his legs.

Some students were playing basketball.

Others were walking the track. Some were on their phones.

"No, I—" Mia started.

"I didn't post that picture," Zach said. "My account got hacked. I tried to take it down. I couldn't. I told Instagram. But they have a whole complaint process. It's crazy. So if you're gonna yell at me, don't bother."

He stared at her fiercely. His lips were moist. His glasses were foggy. Still, Mia could see the sincerity in his eyes.

"Okay." Mia swallowed. "I'm sorry about what happened before."

"For calling me ugly?"

"Yes."

"For saying nobody likes me?"

"Yes."

Mia didn't remember saying those things. Maybe she had said them because she was angry. But she knew that wasn't it. She was mean. That fact made her sad.

She never thought about anybody but herself. She didn't think about the impact of her words.

"Okay." Zach smiled. "Apology accepted."

"Just like that?" Mia was startled.

"Sure. There's no point in being mad at somebody. Especially after they apologize."

She didn't feel that way. She liked being mean. She liked making people feel bad. She really thought she was better than everyone. It made her feel powerful.

"You're letting me off easy," she said.

"Why wouldn't I? We used to be friends, you know."

"We did?" She hoped she didn't sound as surprised as she felt. "When?"

"Kindergarten. You were in first grade. Our class was a combo. You were really nice then."

"What happened?"

"You tell me!" Zach laughed. "It all started when I was in first grade. You were in second. I tried to talk with you. You blew me off. I always saw you with Cassidy and Nicole. You talked with the older kids. But not your old friends."

"Oh." Mia didn't remember talking to him. She just remembered thinking he was a loser. "So, how have you been?"

"Since kindergarten?" Zach laughed again. "I've been okay. I liked fourth grade a lot. I liked Mrs. Lucero."

"Yeah! Me too. She was fun."

Mia had liked her class too. They were always doing cool science experiments. And every student in class got to bring their pets to school for a day. Mrs. Lucero was always trying to teach them with hands-on projects.

"I like middle school way better," Mia said. "I can't wait till I go to Ocean."

"I'm nervous about it." Zach looked at the ground.

"Why?"

"Things changed so much between us. I think it's gonna be way worse when we're older. Like in high school."

"Isn't change good?"

"I don't know." He looked her in the eyes. "How do you like it? You've had a lot of change in twenty-four hours, right?"

"Yeah." She looked away.

The bell rang. Then she had a thought. It came into her mind so quickly she blurted it out.

"You wanna go the Zombie Dance together?"

"Say what? You want to go with me?" Zach put his iPad away.

"Yeah." Mia had absolutely no idea why she said it. But it seemed like the right thing to do.

"Okay. But let's just go as friends." Zach stood up. "I don't want to break your heart or anything." He smiled and walked away.

Mia walked toward the arts building. She had English fifth period. Hmm. She thought Zach would be more excited. She was doing him a favor by going to the dance with him. He didn't see it that way. This threw her off.

As she went to class, she passed the Scabs. They eyed her. Laughed. And pointed.

Then it hit her like a ton of bricks.

The Scabs had doctored that image! They posted the photo!

CHAPTER 10

THAT WAS WEIRD

Mia had thought Lori, Viet, Logan, and Tom were nothing. Nobodies. They were so insignificant. She never thought them capable enough to fake the photo.

I am so lame, she told herself. *Just because I'm smart doesn't mean other people aren't.*

Then she realized she had messed up. Big-time! She was now going to the Zombie Dance with Zach.

Zach!

Mia shook her head.

Calm down. It's a PR move. Total crisis management, she told herself.

She figured kids would see them together. They would realize she wasn't so stuck-up.

Well, she was. But it would look like she wasn't.

Perception is reality, she told herself.

She stopped thinking about Zach.

Mia focused her attention on the Scabs. The losers who had ruined her life.

During English, she wasn't able to think clearly. She had one agenda.

Revenge.

First she imagined herself Avengers-style. Taking down the evil Scabs one by one.

Then she imagined getting in their faces. The Scabs would try to blow her off. Mia had her arguments down. She crafted fantastic insults. The Scabs would cry in front of everyone.

No matter what, she would be back on top. She would rule the school again.

Then Neil would come to her. He would beg her to go to the Zombie Dance. She'd go with someone else. Naturally. Maybe the star football player from another high school.

Anybody but Neil. And of course not Zach.

"Mia?" Mrs. Flores smiled at her.

The class was discussing *Romeo and Juliet.*

"Yes?" Mia asked. She hoped she didn't sound clueless.

"I was asking the class why two people from different worlds couldn't be together."

"Well, um …" Mia was thrown off. It seemed like every eye in the room was on her. She had to say something. Then she had an odd thought. She wasn't too sure about it. And just like asking Zach to the Zombie Dance, she blurted it out. "Why can't they be together? Even though they come from different places. Why should that stop them from being together?"

Everybody stared at her. Mia's heart sank. She knew she probably sounded crazy.

"Go on," Mrs. Flores said.

"I guess … if you like, or love, somebody … Well, why should any of that really matter?"

Mia heard herself say it. Then she realized it wasn't too weird. If two people liked one another, all of the other stuff shouldn't matter. Right?

"Very good, Mia."

Mrs. Flores smiled and nodded at her.

Mia felt something. She couldn't quite pinpoint what it was. She thought about the Scabs.

Why would they want to hurt me? Because we are from different places? Because I have more than they do?

Then it hit her.

Oh. My. God. I've always been self-centered. I've never acted any other way.

She couldn't believe she was thinking like this. She thought her brain might explode. She couldn't believe she cared about how she acted toward others. How what she did and said affected her peers. Her parents. Her friends.

Can I be a good person? Am I even capable of it? she wondered.

According to Zach, she had been acting like this for a long time. Since second grade!

Wait! What if I can't change? Oh no.

The thought scared her.

Way more than the Instagram craziness.

Way more than her shattered status.

As the class discussion moved on, Mia discreetly checked her phone.

No calls. No texts.

She eyed the huge scratch. The way it ran along Neil's face. Looking at it no longer made her feel good.

It's just a phone, she thought.

A phone had started this.

If Mia hadn't been right behind the basketball hoop. If she hadn't snitched on the Scabs. If she hadn't thought of them as Scabs at all …

Mia scrolled through her photos. She found a nice one of her, Cassidy, and Nicole. They were sitting on the cool bench. They were making fish lips for the camera.

She made this the new image on her home screen. She stared at it.

Then she scrolled through her photos again. She found another one. It was a selfie with her parents. Corky was in her father's lap.

She made that her new home screen image. The jagged scratch was now running across her face.

She didn't mind too much.

It was just a phone.

Mia didn't have time to talk with the Scabs after school. She made her way through the school. But she didn't see any of them.

She was relieved. She didn't exactly know what she would say. She had been so sure of herself.

Now? She doubted everything.

Who was I to treat everyone so horribly? Wait! Am I being too hard on myself?

Her thoughts made her more confused.

Zach came up to her at the front of the school.

Oh no! Mia thought. *He thinks I'm into him. He's a total fatal attraction.*

"I got an idea," Zach said. He didn't stand too close. He didn't try to put his arm around her. He was just ... normal.

"Okay. What's the idea?"

"That Instagram picture? I can show everybody it's fake. That we never kissed," he said.

Mia relaxed. Was Zach really a fatal attraction? No. He wouldn't try to prove the photo was phony.

"I'm so lame," she said out loud.

Zach looked at her. She couldn't believe she had just said that.

The queen of Marina Middle School admitting she was lame in public!

"No, you're not," Zach said. "You're just trying to figure this out."

"Figure what out?"

"Being a teenager. Middle school. I don't know. I'm really smart. But I don't have all the answers." Zach smiled.

They continued walking together. Normally, Mia would have gagged at the thought of being seen with Zach.

But it seemed natural. She didn't even think about it.

"I'm sorry for ignoring you all these years," Mia said. She meant it. She didn't know what she could do to make up for it. It did make her feel better if Zach knew she was sorry.

"It's okay. Your loss." He smiled again.

Mia realized Zach had quite a sharp sense of humor. For a nerd.

"I guess so," she said. "And, Zach? Don't be worried about high school."

"Why not?"

"Nice people like you don't need to change. But people like my friends and me? We need to be different."

CHAPTER 11

WAIT A MINUTE

From the moment Mia woke up, things were different.

It started with Corky resting his brown furry body at her feet.

Scratch that. This was normal.

She opened her eyes. But she didn't go for her phone. She stretched. But she didn't do anything else. She just lay in bed for a moment and stared at the ceiling.

This has been the weirdest week! she thought.

For a second she got nervous. Every day since that photo posted, she'd been on a roller coaster.

She missed Cassidy and Nicole. But she knew that wasn't what really bothered her. Her classes would always keep her busy. There was tennis after school. She received an allowance when she did chores.

Do I want to be popular anymore? she asked herself.

It was a lot of work. She hadn't realized how much. She had always been cool. People had always liked her.

But had she always been mean? She didn't know.

On top of that, she lost Neil. He'd dumped her over a stupid photo. *A picture that's not even real,* she reminded herself.

She got out of bed. And realized maybe she was okay with her life being different.

Maybe I don't need to be the coolest. Maybe I can just be me. Normal.

She got ready slowly. She was wrapped up in her thoughts. There was no time to find her friends. Late for school, she ran to class. She didn't look at the cool bench. Not once.

At snack break, she went to the library. She didn't even think about it. She had to find a book on volcanoes. She was supposed to start a report for science two weeks ago. Instead, she'd spent the time texting Neil.

What a waste that was, she thought.

At lunch, she got her bag from her locker. She walked over to the cool bench.

Then her heart sank.

A projector screen had been set up. The Instagram photo of her and Zach was on it. Ugh! What now?

Students were gathered around it. They were laughing. More and more were stopping to gawk at the screen.

Cassidy and Nicole were there.

The Scabs were there.

Rand, Donovan, and Jeff were hurling insults at Zach.

Zach was sitting on the bench. He had a laptop. It was connected to the screen. The screen everybody was looking at.

"What are you doing?" Mia cried as she ran over to him. "I tried to be your friend! And you play me like this?"

Her mind went into overdrive.

She was going to delete all her social media accounts.

She was going to switch schools.

Maybe even change her name.

"Calm down, Mia." Zach eyed the crowd. People were still walking up.

"Calm down? How can you tell me to—"

"Because," Zach yelled. "I want everybody to know you can't always trust what you see online."

The kids quieted down. Some were still laughing.

Zach pressed a few buttons on his laptop.

Suddenly, Photoshop opened. He pressed more buttons.

There was the fake photo. He broke it up into different images. Mia and Zach's faces separated. Everybody could see how it had been doctored.

Kids clapped. They continued to laugh.

They started chanting, "Fake. Fake. Fake. Fake."

"Those pictures are from old yearbooks," Mia said excitedly. "Why didn't I realize that?"

"Because you were so mad." Zach grinned. "The ones of me are from my Facebook page."

"You're on Facebook?" Mia realized she probably shouldn't sound surprised. Or snotty.

"Isn't everyone?" Zach unplugged his laptop from the screen. "Anybody who knows Photoshop can make a fake picture. Just. Like. That. See ya, Mia."

Mia watched as everybody walked away. Nobody was looking at her anymore.

Nobody was laughing. She sat down at the cool bench. Then ate her lunch.

CHAPTER 12

OKAY, CALM DOWN FOR REALZ

Mia realized she was angry.

She couldn't believe how a fake photo had caused so much trouble. It was stupid for anybody to care about who she was kissing.

But she hadn't felt like this before. These thoughts were new. She was used to feeling the opposite. She was used to caring about what everybody thought. She was used to thinking bad things about people. She was used to saying bad things about them.

She was mad at everybody. They had judged her.

They had all seen a photo. Then made a snap judgment. They assumed it was true.

And it wasn't even a big deal, she told herself before sixth period.

Mia spotted Viet and Lori. They were across campus.

Then she realized why she was mad. Who she was mad at. She could blame everyone for her recent problems.

But she knew who was to blame. She was.

Ann looked nervous. It was time for tennis. She walked onto the court. Mia watched her. Coach Austin had put them together today. They were playing doubles.

Mia smiled at Ann. Ann didn't smile back. She didn't even look at Mia.

The game was over quickly. Both girls missed a lot of balls. Mia followed Ann as they walked off the court. Mia picked up her pace. She wanted to walk side by side.

"Sorry," Ann said. She was looking at the ground.

This made Mia feel bad. It was worse than losing. Ann was apologizing. She felt like she had let Mia down. She probably thought Mia hated her.

Why wouldn't she? Mia thought. *I've never been anything but mean to her.* "Why are you apologizing?" Mia forced herself to ask. "You played great."

Ann looked at her. Her eyes were round with shock. "You're not mad?" she asked nervously. "You would've done a lot better. But Coach Austin paired us together. I didn't help us win."

"I'm glad we got to play together," Mia said. The girls sat down to watch the next match. "Hopefully Coach will put us together again."

They talked for the rest of practice. They talked about One Direction. What their favorite TV shows were. Mia even told Ann about Corky.

At the end of practice, they both walked over to their parents.

"Uh …" Ann's nervous look had returned. "Can I ask you something?"

"Sure." Mia smiled.

"How come you're being nice? Did Coach Austin tell you to?"

"No," Mia said. "Let's just say I've had to grow up a lot this week."

"Really?"

"Yeah. I'll tell you about it next time."

"Why wait till then?" Ann took out her phone. "Can we exchange numbers?"

"Sure." Mia smiled. "I'm sorry about how I acted before. I was mean. And it wasn't right to treat you like I did."

Mia took out her phone. She entered her new friend into her contacts.

Mia's mom nodded her head to the radio as they drove home. Mia stared out the window. She remembered how she'd acted last time. How upset she'd been because her mom had bought her a sugary drink. And not iced tea.

"Mom," Mia began. "I'm sorry."

"For what?" Her mom turned down the volume.

"For being a complete idiot. You know. The other day. About the drink you bought. You did something really nice. I was a total brat." Mia leaned over. She put her arm around her mother. She rested her head on her mom's shoulder. "I'm sorry."

"Oh, Mia," her mom said. "I just figured you were being a normal teenage girl."

"Well," Mia said, sitting back up. "Normal teens shouldn't act like that."

She took out her phone. She realized she hadn't checked it much all day. She saw the huge scratch. And the smaller crack. The phone didn't look so bad anymore.

Mia checked for new posts. It wasn't to see

what was happening with the fake photo. She was curious to see what else was going on with her friends. Maybe she had missed something.

She scrolled around. She saw the phony image. She sighed. She really didn't care. *Oh well,* she thought. *Whatever.*

Then she saw some other photos. They were from the presentation Zach had done at lunch. There was even a post showing the two separate images.

Everything's out there now. People can judge for themselves.

Then she got nervous.

What's gonna happen next? Who cares? I can't control what other people think. The only person I can control is me.

IT'S STILL NOT SO BAD

Mia!" Cassidy called.

Mia was walking to first period. The bell hadn't rung yet. She figured she could wait outside the classroom.

She looked over. There were Cassidy and Nicole. Standing at the cool bench. Their phones were in their hands. Mia walked over.

"Where are you going?" Cassidy asked.

"Class," Mia said.

"I love your sweater," Nicole said. She felt the fabric on Mia's arm.

"You look really good," Cassidy said.

Mia didn't know what to think. She didn't know what to do. She hadn't done anything differently. Why were they talking to her now? It seemed sudden.

Even weirder? Cassidy and Nicole were acting like nothing had happened. They had ignored her. Cassidy had stolen her boyfriend.

Don't think about this, she told herself. *Just go with the flow.*

"Why did you guys diss me?" she asked. Mia couldn't help herself. She had changed. She wasn't sure how much.

"Oh, we just thought you were being weird," Cassidy said.

"*I* was being weird?" She wanted to say more. But she didn't.

"Yeah. But things are cool now, right?" Nicole asked.

"Come on … We love you!" Cassidy gave Mia a hug.

Mia couldn't believe it. She had so many questions. She decided to only ask one. "What about Neil? Are things cool with him?" Her eyes burned through Cassidy.

She could see her friend was nervous. Then Mia's body went cold.

Am I gonna go back to how I was before? she asked herself. She was scared. She didn't want to be that person again.

Mean. Rude. Catty. Stuck-up. A total snob. Mia wanted no part of that girl anymore.

"Well, never mind. Who cares about him anyway?" Mia grinned. "I'm just glad to be talking with my besties again."

She hugged them. She realized she must've seemed crazy. But she didn't care.

At that moment the only thing Mia wanted to be was happy.

"What are we going to do about *them*?"

Nicole smiled. She was looking over at two kids. They were standing next to the cool bench.

Mia didn't really know them. None of the girls did. They just knew they were smart. Super smart. This made them nerds.

"Yeah. What are *you* going to do?" Cassidy smirked.

She and Nicole were both excited. They couldn't wait for Mia to give it to the nerds.

The two kids looked up. They saw Mia, Cassidy, and Nicole staring at them.

"Hey," Mia said.

She walked toward the two. And passed them. Cassidy and Nicole followed.

"You didn't do anything?" Cassidy was shocked.

"Nope."

"But … um." Nicole had a hard time putting her words together. "They were near our bench."

"We don't own it." Mia eyed Cassidy and Nicole. "Right?"

"I guess not." Cassidy still seemed surprised by Mia's indifference.

The bell rang.

They followed Mia to her class.

"You guys don't need to walk me," Mia said. "Your class is in the opposite direction."

"Oh." Cassidy seemed surprised. "Okay."

"Did you see that picture of Cody?" Nicole asked. "The one he Snapchatted."

"Yeah." Cassidy smiled warmly. "Hottie McHot."

Mia didn't say anything. She hadn't gotten the photo.

They finished talking. Mia saw Zach in the distance. He was walking to class.

She had a date with him. A date to the Zombie Dance. What would people think when they saw them together?

If it was possible, Mia felt even weirder. She didn't want to be rude to people anymore. She didn't want to be so dependent on her phone. She didn't want others to define who she was.

Still, Zach was Zach. And she was popular Mia. The queen of Marina Middle School. Or was she?

How cool was it to no longer want to be cool?

Mia didn't want to hang with Cassidy and Nicole at lunch. She wasn't mad at them because of what had happened. She felt different.

The Instagram photo had caused a lot of trouble. But it was the best thing that ever happened to her. It forced her to change. To realize how wrong she'd been.

She was supposed to meet Cassidy and Nicole at the cool bench. They were going to discuss plans for the Zombie Dance.

But she found herself near Lori, Viet, Logan, and Tom. They were sitting by some lockers. They were as far away as possible from other kids.

The Sca—she stopped—*Don't even think*

about them like that anymore. It's wrong. It's mean. And it's not cool.

The friends saw Mia coming a mile away.

"What?" Lori said. "Are you going to get us in trouble for not having enough school spirit?"

Viet, Logan, and Tom laughed.

"I'm sorry," Mia said. "I'm sorry for how I've always treated you guys. I'm sorry for always calling you by that stupid name. You weren't acting like scabs. But I was."

They all stared at her. Like her friends, they didn't know what to say.

"I know you guys put up that picture," she continued. "I made you feel like outcasts. You got me back. I deserved it. I just feel bad for Zach. He's really cool. That picture made him even more of an outcast."

"Why?" Lori snapped. "Because a loser like him could never be with Queen Mia?"

"Wasn't that your point? To make both of us look bad?" Mia tried not to sound angry. She didn't feel angry. "Well, I'm sorry for how I've been. I don't expect you to forgive me. I don't even expect you to believe me. But I am sorry."

When Mia walked away, she felt better. She still didn't want to hang out with Cassidy and Nicole. She found herself at the back of the school. Zach was there on his iPad.

"How's it going?" he asked.

"It's good. It's really good."

She wanted to talk about the Zombie Dance. But she didn't.

As she left school for the day, Mia checked Instagram. She noticed Zach was following her posts now. Mia clicked on his page.

The photo of them kissing wasn't there. But she didn't feel relief. She didn't feel much at all.

CHAPTER 14

MAYBE IT IS

Mia woke up the next morning. Corky was trying to bury his head under her feet. She didn't check her phone. She just lay there and stared at the ceiling.

"Why do I feel so weird?" she asked out loud.

She didn't want to think too much. She got up. And got ready for school.

"So you're ready for the math quiz?" her mother asked.

"Yeah," Mia said. "Maybe." She wasn't sure

she was. Mr. Dalton gave quizzes every week. "I think I am."

"You don't sound too sure of yourself." Her mom put some pancakes in front of her.

Mia didn't like to eat a lot of carbs. Her mom knew it. Normally, she would've made a snide comment. Pushed them aside. Instead, she poured some maple syrup on her plate.

"Mia," her dad said as he walked into the kitchen. He was wearing his suit. He hadn't fixed his tie yet. "I am so sorry. We still need to get your phone fixed. I've just been so busy. I promise, tonight we're going to get it taken care of."

Her phone.

Mia hadn't looked at it all morning. She hadn't checked her texts. Hadn't checked social media. The only thing she'd done was put it in her pocket.

"It's okay. My phone's working fine as it is." She ate a bite of pancake. She loved maple syrup. "These are delicious, Mom."

"Are you saying you're okay with your phone

not being fixed?" Her dad sat down. Both her parents looked at her like she had three heads.

"Mia," her mom said. "You can't use it with that big crack in the middle of it."

"Mom," Mia replied. "It's only a phone."

"Hi," Mia said to Lori and Viet.

She was walking with Cassidy and Nicole before first period.

"Hey," Lori and Viet said in unison.

"You just said hi to the Scabs." Cassidy was freaking out.

"What's up with that?" Nicole seemed upset too.

"They're not scabs. They're just … people."

"You always called them Scabs before," Cassidy said.

"You *gave* them that name," Nicole added.

Both girls seemed shocked. It was like they needed to remind Mia how to rule the school. They seemed to want the old Mia back.

"Are you talking to them now? What will people think?" Cassidy eyed Mia sharply.

"What does it matter? I'm not better than they are."

"You're not?" Cassidy asked.

"No." Mia laughed.

Cassidy and Nicole smiled uneasily. They were not happy.

Mia felt her phone buzz. She still hadn't looked at it. The only reason she checked it was because things were awkward with her friends. It was Neil.

NEIL: (Hey.)
MIA: (Going2class.)

Mia put her phone away.

"Who was that?" Cassidy asked.

"Neil." She wanted to smile but didn't. "You can have him if you want him. I'm over it."

"Y-y-you … don't want to go out with him anymore?" Cassidy stuttered. "W-w-hat's wrong with him?"

"Nothing." Mia saw Zach walking nearby. He had his backpack over his shoulder. He didn't look like such a geek anymore. His glasses weren't foggy. He didn't drool. "There are other guys."

"Who?" Nicole asked. "Zach?"

Mia wondered if they knew about the Zombie Dance. About her date. She still hadn't told them.

"Do *you* like him?" Mia asked, giggling.

"No."

Cassidy cracked up.

As they walked to class, Mia felt bad. By asking Nicole that question, she had made fun of Zach.

She wondered if she could ever just be nice. She wondered if her initial replies would always be mean. Or if someday her first words would be kind.

Mia walked out of the cafeteria at lunch. She had thought she was hungry. Then she decided she wasn't. She saw Cassidy and Nicole.

They were standing at the cool bench.

She didn't feel the same about anything. Too much had happened. Too much had changed.

"Hey!" It was Zach. He was yelling.

She turned to see what was going on. Rand, Donovan, and Jeff had taken his iPad. Zach was trying to get it back. Kids were starting to gather around them.

"Here you go." Donovan smiled. Then he threw the iPad to Jeff.

"Don't throw it around," Zach cried.

The laughter continued to build.

"Give it back," Mia yelled. She pushed her way over to Zach.

"Oh, look who's defending her boyfriend," Jeff said.

Everybody laughed.

"Look who's being a jerk," Mia snapped. "Don't you dweebs have anything better to do?"

Rand grabbed the iPad from Jeff.

"We'll give it back," Rand said. "If you kiss him right now."

Kids continued to gather. Mia noticed Cassidy and Nicole in the crowd.

"What's the matter, Mia?" Rand went on. "Scared you'll become a nerd? Be just like him?"

"It's okay, Mia," Zach said. He tried to smile. "You don't have to do this. You can go back to being cool again. It's only an iPad, right?"

Mia looked at Rand.

"You're not gonna kiss him." Rand was sneering. It made him look ugly. "She's not gonna kiss him. Nobody's ever gonna kiss Zach the nerd!"

Then Mia turned. She grabbed Zach and gave him a kiss. It wasn't long. But it was long enough.

Hmm. This isn't bad at all, Mia thought.

The crowd's laughter soon turned to cheers.

Mia grabbed the iPad. Then gave it back to Zach.

Principal Lyon walked over. Everybody started to walk away.

"Is everything okay over here?" she asked.

"Yeah," Zach said.

"Everything's fine," Mia agreed.

The principal looked around. Then she walked away with everyone else.

"Thanks, Mia." Zach was glowing. "You were my first kiss."

"No. Thank *you*, Zach. We're gonna have a great time at the Zombie Dance." She gave him a hug.

Mia took Zach's iPad. She opened up the Notes app. She started typing.

"What are you doing?" he asked.

"Giving you my number. We need to make plans for the dance."

"Oh yeah." Zach smiled. "I gotta go to the library. I'll text you later, Mia."

"Okay." Mia grinned.

Cassidy and Nicole walked over to her.

"That was epic," Cassidy said.

"You showed them all," Nicole said.

"So are you, like, totally into Zach now?" Cassidy asked.

"I guess he's kinda cute. In a dorky way," Nicole said.

"He's not a dork. He's just into different stuff," Mia said. "And as for being into him? I don't know. Maybe."

They watched Zach as he walked to the library.

CHAPTER 15

COOL WITH IT

Mia ended up eating lunch with Cassidy and Nicole. They even sat at a table. Not at the cool bench where they usually ate.

The bell rang. They started walking to their classes.

As they went, Mia noticed something different. She no longer felt like there was a wall between them and everyone else. She didn't feel like she was on display. She didn't feel like school royalty.

And it wasn't bad.

Lori and Viet walked past them. They stopped walking when they saw Mia.

"Hey," Mia said.

"Hey," Lori said.

"Hi, Mia," Viet said.

"Sorry about that picture," Lori said. "We tried to take it down. But it got all those likes. And we had to go through a lot with Instagram."

"We apologized to Zach too," Viet said.

"So it was you guys!" Cassidy said.

"Talk about invading people's privacy," Nicole snapped.

"It's cool. I'm glad you did it," Mia said.

"You are?" asked Lori and Viet.

"Yeah, it ended up showing me what's really important."

"Oh, really? That's rad. Well, see you around," Lori said. The two girls started moving away.

"Do you guys know Cassidy and Nicole?" Mia asked before they were gone.

"Yeah, sort of," Viet said.

"I think we used to play together in elementary school." Lori laughed.

Cassidy and Nicole laughed too.

The five girls walked together. As they went, they talked about the past, present, and future. They were excited about high school. Lori was even looking forward to college.

Here we are, Mia thought. *Five middle schoolers who don't care about being cool.*

Mia's phone buzzed. It was Zach.

ZACH: Thanks again.

Mia stared at it through her damaged phone. *Maybe I could be into Zach. Time will tell.*

She decided right then not to get her screen fixed.

I wanna keep this phone, she thought. *I don't ever want to forget this week.*

WANT TO KEEP READING?

9781680211115

Turn the page for a sneak
peek at another book in the
White Lightning series:

IGGY

CHAPTER 1

COYOTE AVENUE

The plane jerks. I open my eyes. "Ignacia Suarez?"

The flight attendant smiles down at me. So does the jolly plastic Santa pin on her collar. "We'll be landing in Las Vegas in ten minutes. Stay on the plane until everyone else is off. Then someone from the airline will meet you. They'll take you to baggage claim. Okay?"

"Okay," I answer.

She continues up the aisle, collecting trash.

I sit up straight. Look out the window. The ground is flat and brown. So different from Oregon. I wish Dad hadn't moved so far away. And to Nevada of all places.

"I'm sure you and your stepmom will get along fine," says the woman sitting next to me. I'd told her why I'm flying alone. I'm spending winter break with my dad and new stepmom.

I let out a shaky breath. "I hope so."

"Remember, she's as nervous to meet you as you are to meet her. I'm sure they've got your holiday all planned out. You're going to have a great time."

I hope she's right. "What were those places you said before? The fun things to do?"

"Well, let's see," she says. "There's the Big Apple Coaster. Adventuredome. The Big Shot ride. Adventure Canyon. Your parents will know where to go."

It sounds like fun and makes me feel a little

better. Maybe this won't be such a terrible winter break after all.

"Iggy!" Dad waves from baggage claim. He looks a little heavier. But otherwise the same. Five foot seven. Pizza-crust-colored skin. Thick black hair.

"Hi, Dad."

He lifts me off the ground. Grips me in a bear hug. "It's so good to see you. I can't believe it's been over a year."

"Yeah." He feels good. Smells good too. Lime aftershave, just like I remember.

I wish he didn't have to set me down. But he does. Now I'm face-to-face with Tiffany. Dad sent me pictures. But seeing her is still kind of a shock. She's tall. Thin. Blonde. The complete opposite of my dad. Opposite of everyone in my family.

Tiffany is wearing a stiff white shirt. Her hair poofs out like a blonde helmet. The only parts of her body not at attention are her eyes. They sag at the ends. It's like she's already tired of me.

"Hello, Iggy. It's nice to meet you." She sticks her hand out.

"Hi." I shake her bony fingers.

"Your father has told me so much about you."

I have no idea what to say. *It's not nice to meet you. You should have left my dad alone. Given him time to get back with Mom.* I don't say anything.

Dad clears his throat. Takes my suitcase. "Okay. Let's go."

We drive forever on a freeway. Then another freeway. Then down lots of streets that all look alike. We pass houses that all look alike. Dad turns up Coyote Avenue and pulls into the driveway of a white house. The front yard has one skinny tree. Four spiny cactuses. And a lawn of bright white rocks instead of grass.

"We're here," he says proudly.

I follow them inside. Go through a white living

room. Down a white hallway. Into a white bedroom where Dad sets down my suitcase. "We really want you to feel at home here. Don't we, Tiff?"

"Of course," Tiffany says softly.

Dad gives me another hug. "I'm so glad you're here. Make yourself at home. I have a little work to do." He winks and leaves.

Tiffany smiles awkwardly. Pats my arm the way you'd pat a baby's back to get the burps out. "Go ahead and put your things away. The bathroom's down the hall. Let me know if you need anything." She skips out of there like bees are chasing her.

I call Mom's phone. Get her voice mail. "I'm here."

Then I text my best friend, Sophia.

IGGY: Merry Saturday before Xmas from Las Vegas!

I look around the super-neat room. Just a bed, a dresser, and a desk. Nothing out of place. My bedroom in Oregon has yellow walls. A purple bedspread. I haven't seen the top of my desk since I was three. Which is exactly the way I like it.

This is an alien planet.

I need to get out of here.